Do Not Resuscitate

Maurice Saatchi

DO NOT RESUSCITATE

The Life and Afterlife
of Maurice Saatchi

ERIS
86–90 Paul Street
London EC2A 4NE

265 Riverside Drive
New York NY 10025

Edited and designed by Alex Stavrakas.

Hardback ISBN 978-1-912475-59-9
Paperback ISBN 978-1-912475-71-1
E-book ISBN 978-1-912475-72-8

PART ONE

I
WELCOME TO THE GATES OF HEAVEN

Nice to have you with us. First, a personal message from the governing body to congratulate you on your safe arrival.

We apologise for the delay in reaching your chosen destination and are fully aware of the potential for cultural shock and social disorientation that your present situation presents.

We do regret our inability to provide information regarding waiting times on behalf of border control, who operate and manage our immigration halls. We assure you that we are working tirelessly to avoid long queues.

You'll be pleased to know that your papers are in order, so all that remains is a few final tests. If the test results are positive, you will be allowed to proceed on your onward journey. If, on the other hand, we detect signs of abnormality, you will be taken in for further monitoring and treatment.

Our new reception area welcomes over a million applicants a week. We deal with citizenship, right of abode, entry clearance, leave to remain, registration, settlement status entitlement, lawful presence, and conditions of residence. We assist the governing body in identifying, apprehending, detaining, and deporting unwelcome immigrants.

There are, unfortunately, too many fraudulent claims intended to frustrate proper removal, and we face a backlog of hopeless applicants who threaten to overwhelm our border. Additionally, standard biosecurity checks have proven incapable of stemming the flow of immigration. We therefore asked the scientific advisory department to investigate the accuracy and reliability of conventional techniques for assessing eligibility.

We are committed to providing an inclusive and equitable environment at the border. At the same time, we must prevent the importation, seeding, transmission and spread of infection.

II
WHERE WE SEPARATE
THE WHEAT FROM THE CHAFF

To that end, the Recent Applicants Compliance and Enforcement process will deny entry to those who pose an elevated risk of disruption. Treatment will be dispensed on arrival, and it will be swift, certain, and fair.

Of all the options that were considered, the most effective was deemed to be: separation.

Therefore, all arrivals will now be separated into two groups at the border.

To optimise the effectiveness of separation, we have decided to introduce a mental health test. Our pre-screening for potential troublemakers and for all categories of malintent is immune to human meddling, completely data-driven and evidence-based, and entirely foolproof.

We begin with a few simple verification questions. Please note that you can, at any stage, exercise your right against self-incrimination: 'Prefer not to answer' is not an admission of guilt. If you have done nothing wrong, you have nothing to fear.

Bear in mind, however: any illicit attempts to evade questions will result in immediate removal by our qualified security personnel, and failure to co-operate with the testing procedure may irreparably damage your credibility.

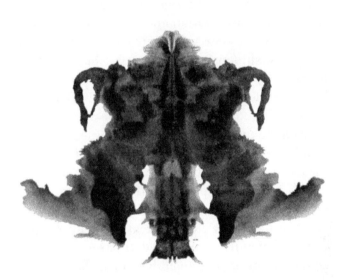

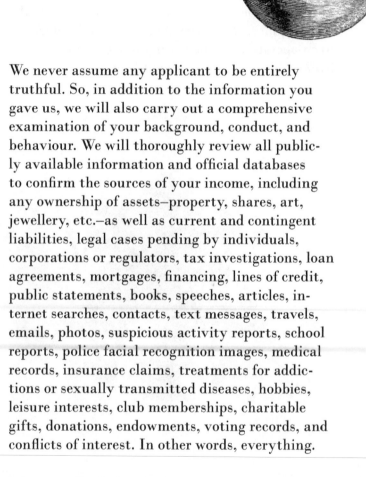

III
HAVE YOU TOLD US EVERYTHING?

We never assume any applicant to be entirely truthful. So, in addition to the information you gave us, we will also carry out a comprehensive examination of your background, conduct, and behaviour. We will thoroughly review all public- ly available information and official databases to confirm the sources of your income, including any ownership of assets—property, shares, art, jewellery, etc.—as well as current and contingent liabilities, legal cases pending by individuals, corporations or regulators, tax investigations, loan agreements, mortgages, financing, lines of credit, public statements, books, speeches, articles, in- ternet searches, contacts, text messages, travels, emails, photos, suspicious activity reports, school reports, police facial recognition images, medical records, insurance claims, treatments for addic- tions or sexually transmitted diseases, hobbies, leisure interests, club memberships, charitable gifts, donations, endowments, voting records, and conflicts of interest. In other words, everything.

IV
A WORD ON PROCESS

Pay attention. You will be assigned a personal R number. To qualify for entry an R number of less than 1 is required. "How is R calculated?", you ask. Here is the sophisticated algorithm we use:

$$R = \frac{\text{Time to default x Amount of default}}{\text{Likelihood of default}}$$

R enables us to profile applicants with just one simple question.

Are you still with me? Here comes the question on which the outcome of your application, and with it your entire future, depends:

Did You Or Did You Not Try To Change The World For The Better?

If you did, you will be granted entry. If you did not, you will be expelled. It's that simple. No ifs. No buts. No grey area. In or out.

V
THERE ARE ONLY TWO
DISTINCT TYPES OF HUMANS

The R test confirms that human beings come in all shapes and sizes, and of course colours, but only two distinct character types. These two types are not only different; they are incompatible. Irreconcilable. Contradictory. At odds. Opposed. Mutually exclusive. Let's just say they don't get along.

More than that, neither can fathom, or accept, that the other exists, that another human being can be so differently constituted. Therefore, the governing body has decided to keep them apart. Forever.

Now you will be asked to identify which group you fit into. Here are some personality traits typical of each category, to assist you with your self-assessment:

IN

- When you come to a wall blocking your path you say: "Let's climb over it. Or go round it."
- You believe that your role is to bring about what would not occur without the intervention of someone like you.
- You think highly of Oscar Wilde, who said: "A map of the world that does not include utopia is not worth looking at."
- You admire Henry Ford, who quipped: "If I'd done what they asked me to do I'd have built faster horses."
- You agree with Tennessee Williams, who wrote: "I've met many people that seemed well-adjusted, but I'm not sure that to be well-adjusted to things as they are is to be desired. I would prefer to be racked by desire for things better than they are, even for things which are unattainable, than to be satisfied with things which are."
- You think there is much that is objectionable about the state of the world. You think that, by an act of will, people can make things better.
- You regard self-determination, individuality, independence as the most prized virtues.
- You believe nothing is impossible, or forbidden, in the process of making the world a better place.

OUT

- When you come to a wall blocking your path you think: "Meh. Too high. Let's turn back."
- You value conservation, stability, order. You are content to be the night watchman.
- You hand back the property in good condition–perhaps better than you found it.
- You reject the heroic view that an idea is worth a thousand armies. You mistrust grand theories, visions, and blueprints.
- Confronted with calls to state 'your aim', or 'what you stand for', you instinctively recoil. You flinch.
- You meet calls for change with a world-weary shrug of the shoulders.
- You trust the wisdom of the Duke of Cambridge: "It is said I am against change. I am not against change. I am in favour of change, when it is necessary. And it is necessary when it is unavoidable."
- You agree with Edmund Burke, who advised you to concentrate on: "What is, not what should be."
- You side with Quintin Hogg in the 1950s: "All the great evils of our time have come from men pretending that good government could offer utopia. We should die rather than sell such trash."
- You are satisfied with the status quo. You are satisfied, period.

For ease of reference, we have prepared this
Handy Guide To Who's In And Who's Out:

IN   **OUT**

CHANGE THE WORLD   DON'T ROCK THE BOAT
EXPLORER   STICK IN THE MUD
CONCERNED   COMPLACENT
ROMANTIC   REALIST
NEW   OLD
WARM   COLD
UNUSUAL   ORDINARY
VISIONARY   PRAGMATIC
INNOVATIVE   CONFORMIST
MOVEMENT   INERTIA
DYNAMIC   STATIC
YES   NO
STAR   STAND-IN
UPFRONT   NO-SHOW
LEADER   FOLLOWER
BOLD   SAFETY FIRST
ODD   EVEN
INQUISITIVE   RELAXED
AN EYE FOR AN EYE   TURN THE CHEEK

VI
AND FINALLY

The Book of Life was opened
and the dead were judged by what
was written in the Books according
to what then had done.

The truth of each man will be laid bare,
and each person who has ever lived will be judged
with perfect justice, going to everlasting bliss,
and going to everlasting condemnation.

Here we present you with a recently commissioned illustration of what the outcome of your application used to look like.

Notice the naked bodies of the applicants. Christ is seated high in the centre. The Virgin Mary is supplicating on behalf of the souls being judged. Saint Michael is weighing the scales and directing the saints and angels around the central group.

At the bottom we see a crowd of souls rising from their graves, being sorted by angels into the saved and the damned. The saved are led up to heaven, shown as a fortified gateway, while the damned are handed over to devils who herd them down to disappear into a hellmouth, the mouth of a huge monster. Isn't it curious: the damned include figures of high rank, their crowns and mitres still on.

We can see that the bodies are then changed: those of the wicked to a state of everlasting shame and torment, those of the righteous to an everlasting state of celestial glory.

But we eventually had enough of this pomposity. We have updated and modernised this whole setup. Now at the far end of the hall you can see two giant screens. The Entry Gate is Green. Hell is Red. This simple traffic light system is the final stage.

Improved detention facilities are now available
to provide unsuccessful immigrants with a safe,
orderly, and dignified onward transit.

We also provide excellent victim support groups
for failed applicants. Our Applicant Re-Settle-
ment schEme is available to all on a first-come,
first-served basis. Outstanding self-isolation and
quarantine accommodation is provided prior to removal, and to our special guests we offer access to
the premium waiting lounge, *St. Peter's*.

We are committed to finding sensible solutions
to any issues that may arise in the course of your
immigration process. A positive and constructive approach is in everybody's interest. Safety is
paramount. Customer satisfaction even more. On
behalf of The Gates of Heaven PLC, we wish you a
pleasant onward journey.

Goodbye, and good luck!

PART
TWO

VII
WE'VE BEEN EXPECTING YOU

SHE

How did you like my new Welcome video? I only finished it last week.

HE

Not exactly friendly, is it?

SHE

The traffic lights were a brilliant touch, no?

HE

Where am I?

SHE

The Library of the Supreme Court.

HE

Impressive!

SHE

The gardens are lovely, aren't they? Thousands of

miles of avenues, lakes, borders, paths.

HE
Makes the Versailles look like an allotment.

SHE
How did your tests go? I want a full report.

HE
A nightmare!
Worse than Heathrow Airport. I thought you
would at least move me to the Celebrity Fast-Track
Channel.

SHE
I couldn't. Wouldn't look good. Wrong optics.

HE
Why am I here?

SHE
You died.

HE
No, I mean *here* here.

SHE
Oh. Your cause of death was 'undetermined'. Your
test results are 'inconclusive'. You're perfect.

HE

Perfect? For what?

SHE

A job.

HE

A job!

SHE

A show trial. You'll be the star. Everyone will be there. Hollywood royalty. Real royalty. The red carpet. The Oscars meets the Nobel Prize. Everyone you've ever heard of. We've been working on it for years. It's all for a good cause.

HE

Glad to be of service.

SHE

It's your big moment. What you always wanted. Your chance to change the world. To make it the way you always wanted. That's been your dream, hasn't it? Now it can come true.

HE

You've gone mad. This is a bad dream. Soon I will wake up.

SHE

Quite unlikely. If all goes to plan, you'll be a hero.
A legend. And we will be reunited forever. It's
not every day you get the chance to express your
views on the world stage.

HE

I couldn't fail to notice you waited until I was
dead. Why did you do it?

SHE

I told you. We needed someone for the job.

VIII
WHAT WILL I HAVE TO DO?

HE

First, let's get some things straight. Who is this mysterious 'we'?

SHE

The Governing Body. Those in charge.

HE

And what exactly do you, or they, want from me?

SHE

All you have to do is win your trial. We'll do the rest. You always wanted to 'arrive'. So here you are. We have the power to make it happen. Spread the word. Send the message to the whole world. We have four billion, and counting, active users. More than Facebook and Google combined.

HE

Not a chance.

SHE

We have the power to deliver a global audience.
Breaking news. A live broadcast, live from here.
Can you imagine? Your message in every school,
mosque, university, synagogue, church, newspa-
per, streaming channel. Best part: no ad breaks.

HE

People don't need me.

SHE

Of course they do. You can help them regain confi-
dence in the belief that they can change the world
and make it a better place. People today have a
lot of problems: inequality, homelessness, poverty,
racism, terrorism, the climate, the Third World
War. They need all the help they can get.

HE

I don't think they do.

SHE

I disagree. You can be of great service to mankind.
You can save future generations from a life of apathy
and boredom. Of disengagement. Of helplessness.

HE

Look, I only died yesterday. Could you please just
let me rest in peace?

SHE

People are confused. Directionless. Lost. Insecure. Your trial can clear the air.

HE

I said, forget it!

SHE

Fine. If you have nothing more to say, then just be a good boy and run along to oblivion.

HE

Go to hell.

SHE

Maybe you'd like to take a look? It's just down the road. I'll show you the way.

HE

No thanks.

SHE

So?

HE

I at least need to know who's on the Jury.

SHE

A representative cross-section of our community.

IX
A JURY OF ONE'S PEERS

X
YOU ASKED FOR THIS

HE
OK, I'll stay. I asked you to come and get me. Not to actually kill me.

SHE
There's no use crying over spilt blood.

HE
This is First Degree murder, you know. Deliberate.

SHE
Legal niceties.

HE
How did you do it?

SHE
Don't you remember? You were having tea in the House of Lords. It wasn't a graceful fall. You just missed your head on the carved oak panelling of the Peers' Guest Room bar.

HE

Then what?

SHE

CPR was administered. Black Rod put you in an emergency ambulance to St Thomas' Hospital.

HE

And then?

SHE

A DNR notice was hung on your door. You were detached from your drips and feeds and monitors. A bowel extractor was fitted. They followed standard procedure.

HE

DNR?

SHE

Do Not Resuscitate.

HE

The doctors said I was dead?

SHE

Well, you looked pretty bad. You were unconscious for twenty minutes.

HE

Was I really dead?

SHE

You might have been in a coma. It's sometimes hard to tell the difference. Doctors are only human you know. We had complete control the entire time: Heart rate. Body temperature. Blood pressure.

HE

What did it say on my death certificate?

SHE

Natural causes—naturally. We're not amateurs. These things happen. Alive one minute, dead the next. 'Sudden cardiac arrest'. It's well described in the medical literature. The blood suddenly stops flowing to the brain and other vital organs. It usually causes death if it's not treated within minutes.

HE

And after my death?

SHE

You were a bed blocker. They needed your room
for another patient. So your body was transferred
to the hospital morgue and put in a freezer drawer.

HE

Is that where you came to get me?

SHE

Yes.

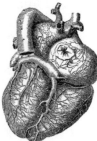

HE

You staged my death! The whole
damn thing. Did you have to do it
in front of everyone in the House of Lords?

SHE

The perfect spot, I thought. All the Presidents
of the Medical Royal Colleges in attendance.
Paramedics in seconds.

HE

Are you saying I wasn't even ill? It was a set-up
from the beginning?

SHE

We don't interfere with the life and death process, unless it is necessary. This time it was necessary. Sometimes it's cardiac arrest. Or a brain seizure. Occasionally, a lightning. Cancer is too slow. We don't mess around.

HE

Cold. Blooded. Murder.

SHE

Assisted dying! There are many ways to serve the Lord.

HE

I was the fall guy. You could have resuscitated me.

SHE

We don't really do resuscitation. Resurrection is more our thing.

HE

This is a joke. Just put me back in my grave and we'll forget the whole thing.

SHE

You missed the boat on that one. Your trial has begun. There has to be a vetting process. Otherwise every Tom, Dick and Harry could get in.

HE

Are you a member of this Governing Body?

SHE

More of a field operative.

HE

And whose field are you operating on today?

SHE

Yours.

HE

What's all this got to do with me?

SHE

We needed a volunteer. I recommended you. From
an excellent pool of candidates, I might add. But
you've been under a lot of strain lately. What with
my death. And your own. So if you're not up to it,
I'm sure we can find someone else. I can always
put you back in the morgue and shut the drawer.
We can forget about the whole thing.

The cleaners will hear you breathing in the morning. A miraculous resurrection. Risen from the
dead. You could go global: The Man Who Cheated
Death! A viral celebrity. Instant fame and fortune.
And you could sue the hospital. I hear there's big

money in medical malpractice claims these days.

HE
Who knows about all this?

SHE
Only the Governing Body. Top Secret. Highest
security classification. Very hush hush. For your
eyes only. That sort of thing.

HE
You thought of everything. You don't seriously
expect to get away with this, do you?

SHE
That's the way it is. Live with it.

HE
But I'm dead.

SHE
We all have to be sometime. And, anyway, you
asked for it. You said you didn't have a life.
Only an existence. You were always moaning
and groaning about how miserable you were. In
the day you dreaded the night. In the night you
dreaded the day. You were in poor shape. You kept
saying "Come and get me". Prayed for a reunion.
So we decided to make your wish come true.

HE

Thanks. A bit ruthless, isn't it?

SHE

You should have thought of that before. It's a bit late now. You'll be reborn. A new man. Fitter and stronger than ever. You'll see.

XI
A SECOND CHANCE

HE

Can I have a coffee, please?

SHE

We don't drink.

HE

Or something to eat?

SHE

We don't eat either. Obviously, you are upset. It's
only natural.

HE

Upset! Are you joking!

SHE

It's always ME, ME, ME with you, isn't it? You're
worse than ever.

HE

That's so unfair! Why do you say such things!

SHE

Do you have any idea what I had to do to get you in here? The planning involved.

HE

Wait a minute! Just a second! What is this? After all I've done!

SHE

Done for who? You!

HE

It's absurd! I thought only of you!

SHE

Of me? You thought of nobody and nothing but yourself. You didn't even know other people existed.

HE

That's such a lie! What exactly is your problem?

SHE

You are my problem. Remember. I'm the one who got you out. Although why anyone would want to spend eternity with you is a mystery.

HE

Better late than never I suppose.

SHE

I was there within a minute. What more do you want? You weren't even cold. If it wasn't for me, you'd still be on a slab in the hospital morgue, stiff as a board. Rigor mortis it's called.

HE

Did I forget to thank you?

SHE

You're being given a second chance.

HE

The Second Coming! I did well on my first go, thank you. I'm not going to be part of your crummy deathploitation plot. I'm out of here.

SHE

Unfortunately, that won't be possible. You're just tired after the journey. Soon we could be having our dream life.

HE

Just like the good old days.

SHE

Or not...

HE

What does that mean? What could be better than that?

SHE

It may be different. That's all. Maybe this time we need a bit more space.

HE

You've had ten years of space. Aren't you pleased to see me?

SHE

Of course I am. You know that. I came to get you, didn't I?

HE

OK, I give in.

SHE

That's the spirit. But first we have to get you through your trial. There are certain formalities. There is nothing much for you to do. We confirm your identity, date, time and place of death, cause of death, last known address, doctor in charge at the hospital.

HE

I don't want this.

SHE

I wouldn't be so picky if I were you. Most arrivals don't even get past the first border check point. A genetic scan will be required.

HE

No thanks!

SHE

It is required. There will be questions about your mental state just before you died. They want to know your motives.

HE

Don't tell me, it's the thought that counts.

SHE

We will have to rehearse the structuring and presentation of complex arguments, providing explanations, referencing, and answering questions. Why don't you pass the time by doing a little reading? Try these:

Balancing Optimism and Rationalism in Immigration Systems

Data Gathering and Predictive Tools in Border Management

Preemptive Screening for Malintent

A Human Rights Analysis of Automated Decision-Making in Immigration and Refugee Systems

The Biometric Border: Sovereignty and Citizenship

Enforcement Alternatives to Detention

Problems in Migration and Free Movement of Persons

HE
You wrote all these. Well done. Forgive me for asking, Miss, but at the end of the day, what's in it for me?

SHE
Me. You and me together. Forever.

HE
I've already got you. You're mine.

SHE
Not necessarily. Now just get on with it. In silence.

HE

Yes Miss. Sorry Miss. Please don't cross and un-
cross your legs like that.

SHE

I warned you before. It's different after you're
dead. Don't try it on again.

HE

It's the stockings. That rustling sound. Do you do
it deliberately?

SHE

Of course not.

HE

Then it comes naturally? The sight and sound of
paradise.

SHE

For Heaven's sake.

HE

I thought you weren't allowed to use that word.

SHE

I have no knowledge of the effect you are describing.
I wouldn't come any closer if I were you. It's called
witness tampering.

HE

From where I'm looking it could raise the dead.

SHE

You are a complete philistine. You're sick. As you
well know, sexual interest wanes with age and
certainly ends after death.

HE

What are you doing now?

SHE

What does it look like I'm doing? I'm getting un-
dressed.

HE

Not on my account, please.

SHE

I have a job, you know. These are my Court robes.
This is my uniform.

HE

Pure white! Beautiful! Reporting for duty, Cap-
tain! All present and correct, Sir. I'm innocent.
Someone must have laid false accusations against
me.

SHE

This is not a Court Martial. There is no firing squad. It's not a kangaroo court, you know. Don't be nervous. Even dead people get butterflies in their tummy. You always said you liked Plato's *Dialogues*. The tension between two people holding opposing points of view 'giving birth' to enlightenment.

HE

The cut and thrust! Thesis! Antithesis! Synthesis!

SHE

Exactly. Systematic dialogue as a method of critical investigation. Expose false beliefs, appearances, and illusions. Reveal unsupported assumptions and misconceptions.

HE

Wonderful! All the drama of the Prosecution and Defence battling it out! Abrupt, rapid questions and answers! Well-honed narratives unravel before the Judge! That's entertainment!

SHE

You've only been here five minutes and you're already making a mockery of our judicial system. Just don't get carried away with your own brilliance. Answer questions politely. Respectfully. Can you manage that? You will be given plenty of time to make a personal statement at the end.

HE

It is sometimes hard to find words to express how wonderful I am.

SHE

Please, be serious. You're on trial for your life. The Judge is waiting. Let's go.

HE

Don't worry. I will give a performance to die for. Knock'em dead! And I will keep a record. The transcript of my trial. Dead simple. My gift to future applicants. We are all asylum seekers in the end.

PART THREE

XII
A DAMNING INDICTMENT

JUDGE
The chaplain will now offer prayer.

CHAPLAIN
Almighty God, give this Court the strength to ascertain of each who would enter, his or her true nature and purpose, lest through oversight there slip into immortality those who would misguide and mislead our people. God save this Honourable Court. Amen.

JUDGE

Let's get started, shall we. The Clerk of the Court will read the Indictment.

CLERK

COUNT ONE! Attempt to fraudulently claim permanent residence for himself by masquerading as an agent of positive change in the world.

COUNT TWO! Attempt to corrupt others into similar acts.

COUNT THREE! Attempt to conceal his true motives and represent himself as something other than what he truly is: an enemy of the people and someone ultimately obsessed with and fixated on one thing and one thing only: himself.

JUDGE

Defendant, how do you plead?

DEFENDANT

Innocent, your Honour.

JUDGE

Very well. Prosecutor, you may make your opening statement.

XIII
THE TRIAL

PROSECUTOR

Your Honour, under your direction, this Court
is always at great pains to show sympathy for
new arrivals. But let us not be blindsided by this
Defendant's case. The Prosecution will provide
compelling evidence of the Defendant's bad character and his propensity to commit offences of the
kind with which he is charged: false or mislead-
ing representations, material omissions, harmful
conduct and associations, and other incriminating
facts that make him an undesirable immigrant.

This Defendant not only seeks entry, he also has
the nerve to ask for reunion with his dead wife!
You know we only want people here who tried to
change the world and make it a better place. The
only change this defendant ever wanted in the
world was a better place for himself. His interest in
change was pure showmanship. A textbook case of
attention-seeking egotism. A class-act of ruthless
calculation to advance his own interests.

Forget all this moralising talk of 'change'. He did nothing out of the goodness of his heart, or because he cared for others. His own wife called him "a selfish, self-centred, egocentric narcissist." We will prove her right. We will prove beyond reasonable doubt that this man was a phoney! A charlatan!

What's more, we do not have to rely on hints and allegations. We will cite specific examples of his misconduct and reprehensible behaviour. Misfeasance. Malfeasance. We will affirm the threat that his infiltration, indoctrination, and subversion pose to our culture, our traditions, and our way of life. Your Honour, a man with a mission is the last thing we need here. He could set himself up as a prophet. A new Messiah. Here of all places!

Defendant, you regarded your own blueprint for a new social order as a crucial insight into the nature of the man. You thought it was the latest and boldest achievement of the human mind, so staggeringly novel that only a few people were sufficiently advanced to grasp it. Correct?

DEFENDANT
I merely answered a calling to change human affairs, to challenge traditional thought. I felt an overwhelming commitment to fairness and social justice.

PROSECUTOR

You saw yourself towering over your puny contemporaries, an omniscient man who contemplated the discomfiture and destruction of the 'philistines'.

But which one of your pools, Defendant, were you swimming in when this revelation about 'fairness' came to you? Or was it on one of the six islands on your thirteen-acre lake—the largest private lake built in England since the Second World War?

Which of your Rolls-Royces, Bentleys, or Cadillacs were you driving around Mayfair when your mind wandered onto the need for more equality? Or perhaps it was in your Riva speedboat, somewhere in the South of France?

Your Honour, at least some people are sincere in their attempts to help the poor. But this one here...

Is it not true, Defendant, that once a guest of yours who was thirsty and needed a glass of water asked you where the kitchen was and you answered: "I'm not sure, but usually they come from over there."

DEFENDANT

But they did!

PROSECUTOR

And isn't it true that when you visited a friend's house, you saw autumn leaves on the lawn and said: "They're so beautiful. Such lovely colours. Where do you get them?"

DEFENDANT

True. And he never told me!

PROSECUTOR

Have you ever been in a supermarket?

DEFENDANT

Not knowingly.

PROSECUTOR

Did you ever wear blue jeans?

DEFENDANT

Of course not.

PROSECUTOR

Have you ever cooked a meal?

DEFENDANT

Never.

PROSECUTOR

Did you ever make a bed?

DEFENDANT

Not that I remember.

PROSECUTOR

The napkins in your house were said to be like tablecloths. Correct?

DEFENDANT

More heavily starched.

PROSECUTOR

You were always served three-course meals.

DEFENDANT

Four, including the canapés.

PROSECUTOR

Your Honour, is there anything worse than someone who preaches about inequality from his hoity-toity life of spoiled luxury? Such hypocrisy! Have you ever made a list of daily tasks or used a planner to structure your time and stay organised?

DEFENDANT

Never.

PROSECUTOR

Have you ever accepted interventions or kept a
healthy sense of perspective?

DEFENDANT

Never.

PROSECUTOR

Did you practise relaxation methods?

DEFENDANT

Never.

PROSECUTOR

Did you ever keep a journal? Or jot down thoughts
or record symptoms? As a constructive way to deal
with pain, anger, fear and other emotions?

DEFENDANT

I never had such symptoms.

PROSECUTOR

Did you ever see a therapist for any of these mental problems?

DEFENDANT

What mental problems?

PROSECUTOR

Problems such as your blatant tendency towards manipulating others and deceiving yourself with excessive self-love. Problems such as believing yourself to be the centre of the universe. Needing others to confirm your identity, wanting excessively to please and impress others. Exhibitionism. Vanity.

Did you ever consider twenty-four-hour in-patient care, hospitalisation, or residential treatment? Or intensive out-patient treatment?

DEFENDANT

I did not.

PROSECUTOR

And there are more skeletons in this closet, Your Honour. Medical records confirm that the Defendant was suffering from memory loss, delusion, paranoia, and confusion. We also have evidence of other conditions: excessive worrying, hair pulling, anorexia nervosa and binge eating, restless legs syndrome, episodes of mania and depression, anti-social and narcissistic personality disorders.

In addition, your test results showed an elevated level of sexual awareness and a low tolerance of sexual frustration. True?

DEFENDANT

So they said.

PROSECUTOR

Your so-called 'love affair' with this dead woman
was just pure lust. Correct?

DEFENDANT

She herself said: "lust is a desire for pleasure".
"Erotic obsession is a desire for union".

PROSECUTOR

Alleyways. Garden sheds. Farmers' fields. The
carpark of the National Theatre.

You used these terms to describe yourself:

Optimistic. Charismatic. Innovative. Risk-taker.
Unstoppable. Dynamic. Determined. Passionate.
Inspiring. Creative. Visionary. Leader. Romantic.
Never say die. Principled. Exciting. Ambitious.

DEFENDANT

Sounds exactly like me!

PROSECUTOR

Your Honour, that was a delusion. According to
extensive polling, this is how others saw him:

Empty talk! Head in the clouds! Pie in the sky!
Eccentric! Flim-flam! Dreamer of dreams!
Troublemaker! Candyfloss! Flights of fancy!
Utopian! Naïve! La-la-land! Waffle! Reckless!
Flaky! Irresponsible! Impulsive! Sensationalist!

And then you went on and applied your selfish
philosophy to British politics...

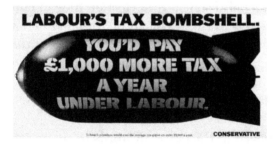

DEFENDANT

I followed the Father: "Do not imagine I have
come to bring peace to Earth. I have come to
bring a sword, not peace."

PROSECUTOR

You were ruthless! Isn't it true that the doyen of
British Election Studies at Oxford University, Professor David Butler, told you that you were 'per-
sonally responsible' for reducing General Elections
to 'negative campaigning'?

DEFENDANT

Negative is not all bad. Nine out of the Ten Commandments are negative. In politics, it is best to
stay strong. "When the camel kneels, the knives
go in."

Politics is an adversarial sport. Hit or be hit. It's not
a world for the squeamish or faint-hearted. It is the
job of a political leader at election time to point out
the defects in the opponent's position. You're in a
boxing ring. Your opponent has hit you in the face.
There is only one thing to do: to land a blow on
your opponent's chin that knocks him out. And it
did. It did and it won four elections in a row.

I believed in the power of words to change the
world. And the fewer words, the better.

PROSECUTOR
Cheap sloganising!

DEFENDANT
Politics is like poetry: the only possible words in the only possible order.

The most powerful rallying cries are simple and to the point: "Your country needs you!" "No taxation without representation!" "One man! One Vote!" There was nothing complicated about: "Liberté. Égalité. Fraternité."

Nobody had to explain what it meant when they read on the Statue of Liberty the inscription: "Give me your huddled masses yearning to breathe free." When they heard: "Go West, young man!" And they did. In their millions.

Nobody needed further elucidation when the Father said: "Do unto others as you would be done by." The average length of the Ten Commandments is seven words.

PROSECUTOR
What mumbo-jumbo. The Defendant's simplistic party tricks are turning this entire Court into a theatre.

DEFENDANT

Simplification is not bad. It serves to crystallise
the issues. A precis is a modern form of good man-
ners. A mark of respect for the listener. Have any
of you read the twentieth century's greatest philosophical work, the *Tractatus Logico-Philosophicus*?
It consists entirely of one-to-two sentence statements.

Has the Prosecution forgotten Mark Twain's opening in a letter to a friend: "I wanted to write you a
short letter but I didn't have time."

Simplicity is the result of extreme technical so-
phistication. Austerity. Concision. It is the goal,
not the starting point. Simplicity is more than
a discipline. It is a test. It forces exactitude or it
annihilates. It precipitates failure when a message
is weak, and it purifies and strengthens a message
that is strong.

One of our Jury members here, Mr. Einstein, has
said that "everything should be as simple as it can
be, and not simpler."

The first British General Election after the First
World War was won by the legendary Prime Minister David Lloyd George with four words: "Homes
fit for heroes!"

PROSECUTOR

Candyfloss.

DEFENDANT

Not according to Lloyd George! He gave his advice to the young Harold Macmillan, the future British Prime Minister, before Macmillan gave his maiden speech to the House of Commons in 1935. Lloyd George explained that after the speech, two Members of Parliament would meet in the bar. One would say to the other: "Macmillan gave a great speech!" The other would ask: "What did he say?" Lloyd George advised Macmillan that if the first man could not give an answer to the second man in a phrase or a short sentence, it wasn't a great speech.

When US President Roosevelt wanted to persuade a profoundly isolationist America to help Britain in her hour of need, he invented a simple phrase to help him do it. He called his policy 'Lend Lease'. And he used simple language to express it: Your neighbour's house is on fire. He comes to you and asks if he can have your hose. You say "I will not give you my hose. But I will lend it to you. You can borrow it to put out your fire. And when the fire is out, you will return it to me". That is how it was done. A simple story of a fire and a hose. The rest is history.

In the post-war 1945 British General Election, Clement Atlee defeated the war hero Winston Churchill with nine words: "We won the war. Now let's win the peace."

PROSECUTOR

Stardust!

DEFENDANT

Delacroix summed it all up: "If a painter cannot capture in a sketch a man falling from a fifth-floor window before he hits the ground, that artist will never be capable of monumental work."

PROSECUTOR

Fancy schmancy words! Childish exhibitionism!

DEFENDANT

Ronald Reagan won his re-election with four words: "It's morning in America."

PROSECUTOR

And let's not forget Reagan's other notable catchline: "Make America great again!"

DEFENDANT

Indeed! Labour won three British elections with one word: 'new'. In New Labour. Britain left the

EU with three words: "Take Back Control". We are not judging the results here, just the undisputed effectiveness of the tools used to achieve them.

PROSECUTOR

Your Honour, the Defendant treated people like morons! He served them simplistic soundbites! He insulted their intelligence. He manipulated the truth. 'Lord Demon Eyes'. That's what they called you, wasn't it?

This man wouldn't know the truth if it was served to him on a plate. He lived, and made others live, on a diet of lies. Lying for a living! In this Court we expect the truth.

DEFENDANT

Not so in politics. Consider a General Election in which the rate of daffodil production is the key issue. The Government would say: "Daffodil production is up." The Opposition would claim: "Daffodil production is lower than when we were in power." The Government would counter: "Daffodil production is the highest in the EU." The Opposition would charge: "Daffodil production is lower than the G7 average." And so on...

In this exchange, everyone is telling the truth. But people know that by the time the matter has been considered over different timescales and different geography, their chances of discovering 'the objective truth' of which party has the best daffodil policy will be limited.

PROSECUTOR
We are not here to discuss daffodils.

DEFENDANT
In politics, even the logical progression,

- Pruning roses is good.
- I prune roses.
- I am good.

fails, because the premise that pruning roses is good is open to question by those who prefer leggy straggly roses with few blooms.

So, man's perception of political good and evil, right and wrong, turns out to be an expression of taste no different to preferring bombe glacée to a bacon sandwich. That is politics.

Tom Stoppard described it: a man standing on the platform at Paddington Station thought he saw the train leaving Paddington, "when all the observable phenomena indicated that Paddington had left the train."

In Man's fallen state after Eden we were denied full knowledge of the truth, which was received only from God. We only got one bite of the apple, not the whole tree.

Our greatest thinkers, here today, confirmed the point.

In Plato's allegory of the human condition, we were tied to chains in a dark cave, able to see a passing parade of objects we thought were real, but which were in fact only the shadows cast by the objects.

Aristotle agreed: Fire burns both here and in Persia. But what is believed just changes before our very eyes. The decision rests with perception.

As Socrates himself explained: You don't know, and I don't know. The difference is, I know that I don't know, and you don't.

PROSECUTOR
Your Honour, is there a limit to how much more of this amateur philosophising we can indulge? The plain truth is that the Defendant has all his life used words for no good purpose other than to attack his opponents.

The Defendant made serious and repeated attempts to stir up discontent and disillusionment
with the established social order. Furthermore, he
did so not out of genuine care for the world and a
burning desire for its improvement, but out of pure
boredom, straightforward spite, egomania, mega-
lomania! You thought you were Chairman of the
World!

DEFENDANT

I was merely advocating change.

PROSECUTOR

Change! Change! Change! That's all we hear from
the Defendant. Mob rule! Anarchist! Agitator!
Disruptor! You thought you were the messenger.
The pulpit. Let me tell you: change for change's
sake is nothing more than disorder. We know from
physics that nature abhors a vacuum. When you
throw the status quo into disarray without anything to replace it you are merely creating chaos.

DEFENDANT

Your Honour, the eye sees further than the hand
can reach. Thwarted idealism and compromised
ideals are the human condition.

PROSECUTOR

He now speaks on behalf of humankind! Self-indulgent eccentricities! A publicity seeker. A loudmouth!

This is not a comedy, Your Honour. We found these in his phone: Brennan's paper "Experiments in the Hypnotic Production of Antisocial or Self-Injurious Behaviour"; Krasnogorski's *Primary Violence Motivation*; Andrew Salter's *Conditioned Reflex Therapy*; Wells's "Experiments in the Hypnotic Production of Crime", and Serov's *The Unilateral Suggestion to Self-Destruction*.

Your Honour, we don't need individualistic outliers to confuse people with alternative visions.

You were preaching Dawnism! Childish dreams of beautiful spring mornings! You were peddling other-worldly talk and distributing material likely to disturb vulnerable young minds with unrealistic images of future heaven.

DEFENDANT

I was just trying to provide a rational assessment of the harsh facts of political life.

PROSECUTOR

Where? In your 'nothing is impossible' fantasy world? You were taking cover under the banner of some kind of democracy movement! You made vague and worthless statements to increase unrest. You said this or that. Whichever way the wind blew. Anything to get attention. You were anti-capitalism! Were you not?

DEFENDANT

Preemptive prefixes had already lost their power: Inclusive Capitalism. Compassionate Capitalism. Caring Capitalism. Enlightened Capitalism, etc. My motive was a fairer distribution of wealth.

 J.K. Galbraith was right: "The greatest restriction on the liberty of the citizen is a complete absence of money." So was our esteemed Jury member, Martin Luther King: "It is a cruel jest to say to a bootless man that he ought to lift himself by his own bootstraps."

I was warning about the consequences of modern capitalism: the creation of giant global cartels beyond the reach of national governments. A huge imbalance of power between the individual customer and the global corporation.

I once asked Margaret Thatcher if she knew the share of the top five banks in Britain in all financial transactions—loans, mortgages, credit cards, insurance—she said she didn't. I told her it was eighty per cent. She said: "It's impossible." She didn't mean it wasn't true. She meant it was intolerable.

PROSECUTOR
You compared British society to the Titanic!

DEFENDANT
Yes! To the Titanic's sinking to be precise. Fifteen hundred people died that night, most of them poor. This was not because the rich passengers were fitter or stronger, but because they were located on higher decks and had better access to lifeboats. The third-class passengers, on the other hand, were less likely to survive because their access to lifeboats was limited. Simple as that. And you know what the crime was: that it was designed to be that way. Deliberate and intentional social eugenics at its purest!

The Covid pandemic revealed a similar picture. Poor people had double the death rate of rich people.

PROSECUTOR
Your Honour, the man is an out-and-out Communist dressed up in the ermine and scarlet robes of the House of Lords.

You, sir, were a closet Marxist posing as a Conservative! Why did you keep this First English Edition of *The Communist Manifesto*?

DEFENDANT

I was fascinated by people who changed the world.

PROSECUTOR

Your Honour, why would any Conservative keep a picture of Marx's tomb in his phone?

DEFENDANT

Because I liked the inscription: "Philosophers have only interpreted the world in various ways. The point, however, is to change it."

PROSECUTOR

You had a fifteen-foot bronze statue of Lenin in your garden. Why?

DEFENDANT

My beloved wife gave it to me as a birthday present.

PROSECUTOR

You were anti-America? Right?

DEFENDANT

I merely agreed with De Tocqueville: "America

is great because America is good. If America ever stops being good, it will stop being great."

America had a fine ideology. But it either forgot what it was or how to express it. A longing for the human dignity that only independence can bring.

Marx himself praised "the New America" as a "classless society" which offered "the greatest possible development of the worker's aptitudes."

Lenin also acknowledged "[t]he war the American people waged against the British robbers who oppressed America and held her in colonial slavery as 'civilised' bloodsuckers."

PROSECUTOR
You criticised the foundations of America's economic success: Google and Facebook! You called them 'data launderers'! Will the Defendant please read out to the Court the outrageous statement he delivered to the House of Lords! This wasn't a speech, Your Honour. It was a sermon!

DEFENDANT
"We want a fairer distribution of wealth and power.

"Big Companies are now worse than Big Government. Welcome to the anthill society. Where at least with Big Governments you could get rid of them every now and then, Big Companies have no fear of removal by the ants.

"Something has gone wrong with Mrs. Thatcher's idea of the 'free market'. It was meant to be a 'perpetual referendum'. People would cast their vote every day, and from the competition to win their custom, better products and services would emerge.

"Unfortunately, it hasn't worked out like that.

"Have you ever tried calling BT? Vodafone? Or UK Power Networks? I have. I timed it. It takes longer to get through to BT than No. 10. Vodafone takes longer than the White House. UK Power Networks take longer than the UK Parliament. And here comes the best part: while you wait you pay. The longer the queue, the bigger their profit.

"Have you ever heard of the people who run these companies? The Chairman perhaps? The CEO? Any board members? Of course not. They are invisible. Anonymous. That's part of the plan.

"Mrs. Thatcher was disappointed to hear that the end-result of competition is the end of competition. She would be horrified to learn that Big Governments now actually prefer Big Companies. The bigger, the better. We love 'em. Yum, Yum. Fewer people to regulate. So much more convenient.

"Finance? Five banks control Wall St. Perfect.

"Defence? In 1990, America had fifty-one 'Prime Defence Contractors'. Today? Five. Satellite suppliers: from eight down to four. Tactical missile suppliers: from eight down to three.

"And there's nothing illegal about any of this. These Big Companies have identical interests. Acting independently, they all automatically do the same.

"Take Google and Facebook. Every time you click on their platforms, you build another swimming pool for a tech billionaire. They are worth $2.8 trillion. More than the UK GDP.

"How did they get so rich? Ninety-nine per cent of their revenue is from advertising.

"They get $250bn a year by selling their 'content' to advertisers. What is their 'content'? You. You are the product they are selling. How much do you get? Zero. It's unfair. Never has so much been taken from so many by so few. Now we want our share!

"Your personal data is priceless. It has created astonishing wealth. The 'data dividend': that has been your gift to them. You created a bigger cake. Now we want a bigger slice. These two companies offer you up as a 'precision-targeted' audience.

"Advertisers no longer have to waste their money selling dishwashers to people who want a shampoo. The tax these two companies pay is not hypothecated in a way that directly rewards those who provided valuable data to these businesses for the value of that data. They have a formidable army. Well-trained. Well-resourced. Its collaborators are everywhere. Seasoned operatives, they are hard to spot, and easily blend into the crowd. They are skilled defenders of their status quo: outwardly normal, productive, sober, and respected members of the community. To avoid suspicion, they play golf and go to the opera.

"We must follow the money. Let us assist businesses that profit from data supplied to them but either cannot find convenient ways of sharing the wealth in that data, or for various reasons do not want to do so.

"I am hopeful this will open the door for more people to participate in the success of these great platforms.

"These Big Companies think they are Big Daddy. To them, we are helpless administrative units with no power or influence. They commit what the Pope calls 'the modern sin. The sin of indifference'. A shrug of the shoulders.

"Perhaps it's time for Sylvia Plath to rescue the ants from Big Daddy:

"Daddy, Daddy, you bastard, I'm through."

PROSECUTOR
You were threatening the great American financial institutions!

DEFENDANT
If you're going to clean house use a bucket and a big mop.

PROSECUTOR
It was mischief-making! Rabble-rousing! Sensation-seeking! You would have received a standing ovation in the Great Hall of the People of China.

DEFENDANT
I was protecting people from free-market capitalism. Capitalism without competition is exploitation. If we are only going to have a two-company market, we may as well go the whole way and have

one-party government.

PROSECUTOR
You were pro-China. Fair?

DEFENDANT
I pointed to two glasses on a table. One glass is made by Company A. The other by Company B. The Chinese State hires professional managers to run these two companies. It gives them a profit target. If they meet it, they stay. If they don't, they are fired. Sounds familiar, doesn't it? The only difference is that the State owns 100 per cent of both companies.

PROSECUTOR
You arranged for the Chairman of the Asian Infrastructure Development Bank to deliver the Margaret Thatcher Lecture. True?

DEFENDANT
As well as Rupert Murdoch, Boris Johnson, and Henry Kissinger.

PROSECUTOR
You welcomed the State Counsellors to the State Council of the People's Republic of China. Correct?

DEFENDANT
They were studying Mrs. Thatcher's economic policy.

PROSECUTOR

But why did China's Minister for Communist Party Affairs tell you at dinner: "If America falls, it's not our problem."

DEFENDANT

I cannot be held responsible for Chinese foreign policy.

PROSECUTOR

You accepted a gift from the Chinese Embassy in London. Correct?

DEFENDANT

A nice box of chocolates.

PROSECUTOR

Glory, Glory, Hallelujah! Unfurl the banners! Sound the trumpets! The Boy Wonder has arrived! Read all about it! A prima donna spreading fake news and alternative facts to subvert democracy by all sorts of intrigues and despicable methods. We have exposed his capacity for brainwashing the people. His double sidedness.

DEFENDANT

Not 'brain washing'. I prefer the term 'dry-cleaning'.

The Prosecution's opinion seems to be that anyone who opposes the status quo is a dangerous radical and a Bad Character.

All of us have dreams. It is a human instinct. And the hope for change can be positive and constructive.

Your Honour, the Prosecution's ship is lost at sea. It wasn't going anywhere in particular to start with; it had no destination or even a compass.

But now it has completely fallen prey to winds and tides and is just circling round and round its precious 'centre ground'. If this is their best shot at me, I am appalled. Nay, worse: I'm disappointed!

The Prosecution forgets that what makes human beings different is that we possess the power of imagination. We can conjure up in our mind a vision of a better world and a better life. When a man or woman stands up for an ideal, or strikes out against injustice, people of all classes and ages are filled with hope.

PROSECUTOR

Childish!

DEFENDANT

Our firmest beliefs are those to which we are

most committed, those in which we have invested everything. Take them away and you take away the keystone of the arch.

PROSECUTOR

Philosophical claptrap!

DEFENDANT

We know more. We know better. In the 1960s, four per cent of us went to university. Now it's fifty per cent. We don't have to rely on the BBC to tell us what's going on. We know it all. We are the most aware and sophisticated electorate in the world. Nobody understands this better than the team inside No. 10 Downing Street. That's why they ask our opinion on everything, every minute of every day. They just keep the results to themselves. So perhaps it's now time for the people's voice to be heard directly.

Your Honour. I wanted every child to know that nothing is impossible. Not to listen to people who say 'it can't be done'. If you try to make any change, you will have people for you and people against you. The alternative, as presented by the Prosecution, is to have nobody for you and nobody against you.

Aristotle provided an easy escape route for the

risk-averse: "Say nothing. Do nothing. Be nothing." But, as he explained, this is a counsel of
despair leading only to oblivion. The Prosecution
never tried to hear "the rustle of God's mantle
passing through history and catch his coat tail for
a few steps."

The Prosecution does not recall the final words of
our distinguished Jury member, President John F.
Kennedy, in the speech he never gave, in Austin,
Texas, the city he never reached, on the day that
never ended, November 22, 1963: "Neither con-
formity nor complacency will do." Like St Paul:
"Always pressing onward to the upwards call."

Your Honour, it only takes a few words to change
the world forever.

The Sermon on the Mount: "And it came to pass,
the people were astonished at His doctrine."

The American Declaration of Independence:
"Whenever any form of government becomes destructive it is the right of the people to abolish it."

The Communist Manifesto: "The proletarians
have nothing to lose but their chains. They have a
world to win."

PROSECUTOR

There you have it, Your Honour. His true character. In the name of 'change' he was trying to overthrow capitalism. The man is an extremist! A militant! He is a terrorist!

DEFENDANT

Your Honour, may I now respectfully make a personal statement to support my application for a reunion?

JUDGE

If you can be brief.

PROSECUTOR

Your Honour! I protest. This is highly irregular! It is outlandish! This is unprecedented!

JUDGE

We are here to set a precedent.

PROSECUTOR

Your Honour, the testimony of a bereaved husband does not carry much weight. Blood is thicker than evidence.

JUDGE

Are you suggesting that the witness would lie?

PROSECUTOR

It has been known to happen. This Court has a long history of emotional lovers drenched in tears.

JUDGE

Defendant, do you understand that reunification is permitted only in exceptional cases, and *only* on extreme compassionate grounds?

DEFENDANT

I understand.

JUDGE

Do you understand, further, that it requires a convincing demonstration of true love? The length of the marriage is irrelevant.

DEFENDANT

I understand.

JUDGE

Are you aware that your deceased wife is now a distinguished legal scholar, the author of the Official Guide to our judicial system?

DEFENDANT

I am aware.

JUDGE

And being so aware, do you still wish to pursue this application for reunion with her?

DEFENDANT

I do.

JUDGE

We require tangible evidence that you met the defined legal standard of true love.

DEFENDANT

I will provide such evidence.

JUDGE

Very well. Continue.

XIV
A MOST HEARTFELT PLEA

PROSECUTOR

Did you love your wife?

DEFENDANT

Yes.

PROSECUTOR

You wrote love letters to each other?

DEFENDANT

Many.

PROSECUTOR

Where are they now? The Court will note that they have not been entered as exhibits to support the case for reunion.

DEFENDANT

There are 1,628 of them in the library. The rest are in our tomb.

PROSECUTOR

In the ten years after her death, did you speak to
the deceased woman?

DEFENDANT

Continuously.

PROSECUTOR

Did you seek her advice?

DEFENDANT

Always.

PROSECUTOR

In connection with the proposed reunion, did you
have episodes of sexual thoughts about the deceased?

DEFENDANT

Regularly.

PROSECUTOR

Did you have any other sexual relationships following her death?

DEFENDANT

None.

PROSECUTOR

Did you remarry?

DEFENDANT

No. After her death, I tried to save her from oblivion.

PROSECUTOR

Marvellous. Did you put a nice picture of her on the mantlepiece? Your Honour, what could possibly be gained by wasting the Court's time with further gory details?

DEFENDANT

My behaviour after her death is a relevant consideration. May I go on?

JUDGE

Please tell the Court about the untimely death of your wife.

DEFENDANT

The day of her sentencing was a warm, bright day.

7.35   BBC *Today* programme: Poetry in schools
10.30 Visit GP for 'tummy ache'
11.30 Sent to Harley Street specialist
12.30 Sent to hospital for scan
13.30 Scan repeated for confirmation
14.30 'Stuff' found

15.30   Sent to waiting room
17.30   Sent to Harley Street for results
17.31   Three words: Malignant. Advanced. Inoperable.
17.32   Sentence pronounced: "...that you be taken from here to a place of execution and there hanged by the neck until you be dead. And may God have mercy upon your soul."

The sentence was carried out a few months later.

I was distressed by the treatment she received for cancer. I claimed it was medieval. Degrading. Ineffective. Drugs? Forty years old. Surgical procedures? Forty years old. Mortality rate? 100 per cent. Survival rate? Nought.

They hit her with a crack. I thought they might as well have shot her there and then and got it over and done with.

Her bosoms turned into dried raisins. Her legs turned into elephant trunks. Her arms turned into a heroin addict's arms. Her hair fell out in handfuls. That was the good news. That was before nausea, diarrhoea, fatigue and projectile green vomiting.

PROSECUTOR
Do you suppose doctors did that to her deliberately?

DEFENDANT

Of course not. They did it because they didn't know any better. Exactly a year before, to the day, I had seen the results of her annual scans. The letter from the consultant in Harley Street read: "I am pleased to tell you your results are normal, including the all-important CA125 cancer test." I was told this was the 'gold standard' in cancer diagnosis. So all was supposed to be well.

PROSECUTOR

Did you have an unsatisfactory conversation with her cancer consultant?

DEFENDANT

There is a record of it:

"DEFENDANT: Is there any more we can do?

CONSULTANT: In your dreams, pal!

DEFENDANT: Can anything else be done?

CONSULTANT: Dream on, chum!

DEFENDANT: Can we attempt an innovation?

CONSULTANT: We must do no harm. We don't want a quack's charter. Patients treated like mice.

Bodies piled high in the streets.

DEFENDANT: One patient can change the world.

CONSULTANT: We want science. Not anecdotes.
We must not waste money on futile efforts that
only raise false hopes.

DEFENDANT: What about genes? Isn't that the
future of medicine? Precision-targeted genetic treatment? Professor Michael Birrer, the Head of Wom-
en's Gynaecological Cancer at Harvard, says...

CONSULTANT: Oh, Michael, yes, he does bang on
about genes. I opened the last Cancer Conference
in Vancouver where Michael presented his human
genome theories. No significance at all.

DEFENDANT: But to help others in the future,
could there be more screening for early diagnosis?
A better chance of survival?

CONSULTANT: Screening is a waste of doctors'
time and public money. One minute you don't have
fatal cancer. The next minute you do. The date of
death is the same.

DEFENDANT: You are administering treatment
knowing it leads only to poor life quality followed

by death. Your 'standard procedure' is turning her into a little sparrow."

Your Honour, could the Prosecution hear my statement without the benefit of sarcastic smiles, grimaces, or expressions of disbelief?

JUDGE
Would the Prosecution abstain from gratuitous facial expressions.

PROSECUTOR
I apologise, Your Honour.

JUDGE
Defendant, please continue.

DEFENDANT
"CONSULTANT: The condition is Stage Three. Of Four. We will perform a 'Radical Re-Section' of her stomach.

DEFENDANT: Thank you, Doctor.

[...]

CONSULTANT: The operation has been a complete success. All clear. All traces of cancer have been removed. Except of course for cancer cells.

We can't see those, of course.

DEFENDANT: Of course not.

[...]

CONSULTANT: Her breathing has changed. She's gone."

PROSECUTOR
What did the Defendant do about it? Did you change the world of cancer?

DEFENDANT
I tried. I took forward a Bill in the House of Lords. With the support of both Houses, friends in the medical profession, the Prime Minister and No. 10's Head of Policy. I hoped future cancer victims might benefit from more innovation, from greater scope to depart from 'standard procedure'. It became an Act of Parliament.

PROSECUTOR
So you changed the law on medicine. So what? That doesn't give you the right to come barging in here with changes to our laws! The nerve of him! Who does this man think he is?

Your Honour, the Defendant looks pale!

XV
ODE TO JOSEPHINE HART

JUDGE

Would the defendant like me to suspend the hearing to allow time for him to recover his composure?

DEFENDANT

No, thank you, Your Honour.

The Dean of Westminster, Dr John Hall, allowed the deceased the unprecedented honour of a memorial poetry reading in Westminster Abbey, beside Poets' Corner. When the Dean was asked whether such an event might be possible, his reply was that it would be 'very appropriate'.

Poets' Corner in Westminster Abbey holds 250 people. I nervously told Sir Stephen Lamport, the Receiver General of the Abbey, that 500 people had accepted the invitation. After a brief pause: "We knew that would happen. We're moving you to the Nave".

So it was that members of her repertory company of great actors—Eileen Atkins, Bono, Kenneth Cranham, Charles Dance, Joanna David, Emilia Fox, Edward Fox, Julian Glover, Jeremy Irons, Felicity Kendal, Damian Lewis, Helen McCrory, Ian McDiarmid, Elizabeth McGovern, Sir Roger Moore, Dan Stevens, Harriet Walter and Dominic West—came to Westminster Abbey for a reading of T.S. Eliot's poems "The Love Song of J. Alfred Prufrock", "Portrait of a Lady" and "The Hollow Men". They were directed by her mentor, Michael Grandage, who, a year before, had told her he could fill the Donmar theatre with her poetry for a week. And he did.

She spoke of her 'absolute respect' for actors, and dedicated her last book to 'The Mysterious Art of the Actor'. No mystery there, Your Honour. Kind people. Generous people. Brilliant people.

For an explanation of her view that poetry is a force for good in a human life, I refer the Court to her Royal Life Saving Institute Certificate, awarded to her age thirteen. The citation reads: "For practical knowledge of rescue, releasing oneself from the clutch of the drowning, and for the ability to render aid in resuscitating the apparently drowned."

For her, poetry was life-saving. She described her relationship with poetry as "a long love affair, which started with a *coup de foudre* in a House of God": "In the beginning was the Word, and the Word was with God, and the Word was God." She said this was the first line of pure poetry she ever heard, and that it remained, to her, perfect.

She learned about God from the nuns of the Convent of St Louis near her hometown of Mullingar, in the middle of Ireland. The nuns taught her to read. Sometimes too well. She was often caught and punished for taking a torch and a book under her bedclothes. The nuns taught her to sing. To her rendition of "Do Re Mi", Sister Columba said: "Sit down child and never sing again."

The nuns taught Josephine Hart a literary hierarchical system of Orwellian precision: Novels good. Plays better. Poetry best.

The nuns showed her the difference between a mortal and a venial sin. When Gregory Peck kissed Audrey Hepburn in *Roman Holiday*, the nuns shook the projector. From the nuns, she learned that confession to God is a shining shield over your chest, to keep you pure and clean. Age fourteen, this is what she wrote: "We stand for God, and for his glory. The Lord Supreme and God of all, strengthen our Faith, Redeemer, Guard us when danger is nigh. To thee we pledge our lives and service. Strong in a Faith that ne'er shall die."

Fifty years later, a week before she died, she received this letter from Professor Kevin Nugent at Harvard Medical School:

"I have a very clear picture of you in my mind. I often saw you in the town, of course, when I was a small boy, but would not have dared speak to you. From my prepubescent vantage point, you were surreally glamorous and unapproachably beautiful.

"But I have had one clear memory of you that has remained with me over the years. It may be a distillation of many memories, but it is now reduced to a memory of one Sunday from the Sundays of my childhood.

"I was coming down past Flanigan's mills on my way to a match—maybe even play in a match—in Cusack Park, when I heard a voice—a projected dramatic even operatic voice—not exactly the flat Mullingar accent I was accustomed to.

"When I reached your house, the bungalow, which I somehow associate with yellow flowers, I saw you in the garden, 'declaiming'. I might even have used that word even then to describe it to myself. You were in a long flowing dress that went down to your ankles, and I think you might even have had a floppy sun hat. But you were in full flight.

"It was clearly a performance, but you seemed so self-contained, that I could see that the performance was for yourself and maybe for whoever else was in the garden on that day, but only for the rest of us if we cared to take it in. I did. I am sure I did not stop in case I would be caught gaping. You were mesmerising.

"That vision lingered for a long time afterwards in my memory and has lasted until today, fifty years later.

"You were so different, so that whenever I heard news about you later—after your St. Louis days—I was not surprised.

"I well remember the night your brother was killed.

"We were playing on the Fair Green, opposite Grand Parade, when we heard the echo of the explosion.

"What I do remember is that we stopped playing and gathered in the middle of the pitch. 'Carbide', one of the older boys claimed. We began to drift home as the game had somehow lost its pull on us.

"There was a sense of uncertainty or foreboding in the air.

"It was only the next day on the way to school we heard the news that your brother had been killed.

"It was too much to comprehend, and no one was able to help us understand it. It was not discussed but it seeped deep into our psyches.

"It was the beginning of a slow realisation that life was not as safe or as predictable as we thought."

On that night, the priest came to her house to ask if she wanted to, or should he, tell her parents that her younger brother had died in the accidental explosion at their house. The last her brother had said to her was: "Turn me over. Don't let mama see me."

So it was that she walked along the corridor to her parents' room. And spoke her last words to God: "I hate you."

She also had definite views about love. She said it is: "The extreme emotion. The incandescent experience."

She was sure that 'dying for love' is celebrated in the iconography of the cross, that: "God had sent His dearly beloved son down to earth to die for our sins. And thus prove His love for us." For her, "Love is sacrifice. And sacrifice is a sign of love." She says her mind was formed "in a benediction of this most beautiful concept."

After the death of her brother, age one, her sister, age eight, and her other brother, age fifteen, her mother was among the last patients to be given electric shocks to erase memory. It was called ECT—Electroconvulsive Therapy. Shortly after the third death, she left Ireland never to return.

She got employment as a teller at the Holborn branch of Barclays Bank. And went to Guildhall acting classes in the evening. The bank manager told her: "This job is not for you."

A few days before her own death, she left hospital

for her last Poetry Hour. Shortly after, I received this letter:

"I am the taxi driver who took your courageous wife to the opening of the poetry week at the Donmar Warehouse Theatre. I have never been so deeply touched by someone's sheer fortitude and determination, and I was totally overcome by this. That chance encounter has changed my view of life."

She respected words. Well, out of nowhere, they finished her with only three words:

MALIGNANT - ADVANCED - INOPERABLE

But I can do better, Your Honour. I will finish her for you. Right here and now. Once and for all. With three much better words:

VIVACITÉ

She was Ladies' Breaststroke Champion of Mullingar, age fifteen. Years later, to see her powerful breaststroke in water is a sight of unparalleled female beauty. The word means: 'The vigour of hardy plants'.

VOLUPTÉ

Beautiful décolletage. Shoulders. Legs. The
boys in Mullingar particularly admired her legs.
They had a phrase for it: 'Beef to the heel. The
Mullingar heifer.'

VOLONTÉ

It means: 'will'. She said poetry, once it entered
her mind, surfaced at times of need, and became
a lifeline. And it did. She said: "For a girl with no
sense of direction, poetry was a route map through
life." And it was.

She said it all started in a House of God. So, here
we are again. "In my beginning is my end."
I respectfully ask the Court to consider granting
us a reunion here in Heaven.

XVI
A HOPELESS RETORT

JUDGE
You may step down. Does the Prosecution wish to respond?

PROSECUTOR
Yes, Your Honour. This is all very touching, but entirely beside the point.

Defendant, is this the tomb you built for her? It has a lead-lined room below for two coffins. One for you and one for her?

DEFENDANT

Correct.

PROSECUTOR

All this bizarre monument building, Your Honour. Why couldn't you just put up a gravestone like everyone else?

This is the library you built for her, inaugurated by the Dean of Westminster?

DEFENDANT

It is.

PROSECUTOR

These are the 450 archive boxes in vellum you made for her works? And 220 metres of shelves for her 7,000 books?

DEFENDANT

Correct.

PROSECUTOR

This is the pyramid you built for her statue, engraved with the titles of her books?

DEFENDANT

It is.

PROSECUTOR

This is Monsieur Cardot's studio in Paris where her statue was designed?

DEFENDANT

Yes. I am pleased to see Monsieur Cardot here with us today.

PROSECUTOR

And this is the statue of her to stand on top of her pyramid?

DEFENDANT

Yes.

PROSECUTOR

His previous works in Paris of Winston Churchill and Charles de Gaulle were unveiled by Her
Majesty the Queen and the President of France?

DEFENDANT

This is all public knowledge, yes.

PROSECUTOR

And did you build a theatre for her?

DEFENDANT

I did. Your Honour, the Prosecution is making a
mockery of grief.

PROSECUTOR

You carved her name in twenty-foot letters across
the hillside in Sussex?

DEFENDANT

I did.

PROSECUTOR

You repeated your honeymoon in Paris? You
returned alone to the same room in the Paris Ritz.
Suite Hemingway, wasn't it? You went to the same

tables in the same restaurants in the same order as on your honeymoon? Laurent. Lasserre. Lipp. Pré Catelan. Hardly a penance, is it?

You laid out her place at mealtimes: plates, glasses, cutlery?

DEFENDANT
True.

PROSECUTOR
And you put flowers at her place every day until your own death?

DEFENDANT
Only for lunch.

PROSECUTOR
You visited her tomb for breakfast every morning?

DEFENDANT
For seven years.

PROSECUTOR
Only seven? How many miles would you say you drove to do that?

DEFENDANT
3,072.

PROSECUTOR

Your Honour. Not a dry eye in the Court. But, Your Honour, we are all too familiar with this sort of tear-jerking sentimentality.

Your Honour. This kind of obsessive behaviour is typical of mental illness. It is classic schizophrenia. Fantasy and reality all mixed up. An almost child-like simple-mindedness coupled with unhealthy exhibitionism. Would you tell the Court what your motive was for all this repetitive ritual and monument building?

DEFENDANT

I didn't want her to be forgotten.

PROSECUTOR

I put the case that this was not your motive at all. I insist that all these grand gestures were nothing more than an undignified attempt to make yourself the centre of attention. Your friends told you to stop all this bizarre weeping and wailing. They said you were just trying to gain sympathy.

DEFENDANT

There was nothing bizarre about these rituals. They were tender rituals. Loving.

PROSECUTOR

Or do you suppose, reflecting upon the loss to the world of such a valuable life as your own, that your final decision was to stay alive? That is called 'narcissism', isn't it?

Your Honour, is there anything more hypocritical than a bereaved man who protests his distress and then does nothing about it? Haven't you left out the most significant non-event of the period? The change that never happened? You continued going to Parliament. You gave speeches. Wrote pamphlets, press articles. You hosted lunches. Attended dinner parties. You carried on as if nothing had happened. You said without her you had a pointless existence. So why didn't you just kill yourself and apply to come here sooner? Instead of waiting for her to do it?

DEFENDANT

The Dean of Westminster, who I loved, explained that in the opinion of the Church of England suicide is a sin. So there would be no reunion and I would never see her again. Until now.

PROSECUTOR

Your Honour, haven't we heard enough of this lovey-dovey mush?

Experts from the Committee of Medical Examiners have confirmed the Defendant's pre-existing medical conditions. He is a troubled person. Deeply maladjusted. Never to be trusted. A loose connection. Crossed wires somewhere.

The Defendant is a destructive, disruptive force who should never be allowed in! He should be sent away! A guilty verdict will be greeted with relief by the entire community.

JUDGE
Thank you. The Court is now adjourned to await the verdict of the Jury.

PART FOUR

JUDGE

The Clerk of the Court will now confirm the basis
of the rulings of this Court.

CLERK

This Court of Decision:

AFFIRMS the commitment that entry to Heaven
should be accessible to all, based solely on merit
and not on gender, race, religion, ethnicity, or sexual orientation.

WELCOMES the full and equal right of all applicants to be treated with rigorous impartiality.

RECOGNISES that following the recent influx of
immigrants, stricter admission tests are required.

ACCEPTS that no human being shall be allowed
to pass through the Gates of Heaven without
compelling evidence that they tried to change the

world for the better.

AGREES that anyone who fails this test will be deported to oblivion and forgotten forever.

ENDORSES this Court of Decision as the final arbiter of all contested cases.

JUDGE

Members of the Jury. Allow me to sum up the case before you. It is up to you to settle once and for all the question at the Gates of Heaven. Who's IN and Who's OUT?

This test case may signal a historic shift in our immigration law. I must emphasise that you do not have to be convinced that the Defendant climbed Mount Everest. Cured cancer. Ended poverty. Or stopped all war. You only have to be satisfied that he or she did at least try to change the world for the better. To qualify for entry a reasonable attempt is all that is required.

The Jury retires to consider its verdict.

Has the Jury appointed a speaker for you all?

JURY MEMBER

Yes, thank you your Honour.

JUDGE

On the question of whether the Accused shall be allowed IN or sent OUT, has the Jury reached a verdict?

JURY MEMBER

We have, Your Honour.

JUDGE

The Clerk of the Court will now request the Jury's verdict.

CLERK

On the first Count, does the Jury find that the Defendant did or did not to the best of his abilities effect a positive change in the world?

JURY MEMBER

He did.

CLERK

On that basis, is the Defendant's application for permanent residence fully justified and approved?

JURY MEMBER

It is.

CLERK

On the second Count, does the Jury find that the

Defendant through his actions and personal behaviour has been a positive or corruptive influence
on others?

JURY MEMBER
Positive.

CLERK
On the third and remaining Count, does the Jury
find that the Defendant's motives were informed
by considerations other than himself alone?

JURY MEMBER
They were.

CLERK
On the whole, does the Jury then find the Defendant Worthy or Not Worthy of Indefinite Leave to
Remain in Heaven as a Permanent Resident with
the rights, privileges, and powers of a full member
of the Community?

JURY MEMBER
Worthy.

JUDGE
Furthermore, does the Jury find that a reunion
with the previously deceased should be permitted?

JURY MEMBER

We do, Your Honour.

JUDGE

Is that the verdict of you all?

JURY MEMBER

It is.

JUDGE

So ordered.

———

And so it came to pass. As they rose up the stairway into the bright, blue sky full of stars, a giant glass bell jar descended over the married couple: an eternal symbol of the fact that a marriage made in Heaven can change the world and last forever.

THE
END

IMAGE CREDITS

BIOGRAPHICAL NOTE

Maurice Saatchi graduated from the London School of Economics, where he won the MacMillan Prize for Sociology. He went on to become a Governor of the LSE. During his time in advertising he transformed the industry, taking Saatchi & Saatchi from an eleven-staff company to being the biggest agency globally. He worked with Margaret Thatcher and John Major on four consecutive General Election victories. In 1996 he entered the House of Lords, and later became Shadow Minister for the Treasury and the Cabinet Office. He became Co-Chairman of the Conservative Party, and Chairman of the Centre for Policy Studies. His campaigning efforts in Parliament led to the passage of the 2016 Access to Medical Treatments (Innovation) Act.

Printed in the USA
CPSIA information can be obtained
at www.ICGtesting.com
JSHW021519010424
60353JS00003B/77

9 781912 475711